WRITER
TOM HUTCHISON

ISSUES 6-9
ART & COLORS - FICO OSSIO
LETTERS - KEL NUTTAL

ISSUE 10
ART - ALISSON BORGES
COLORS - KATE FINNEGAN
LETTERS - KEL NETTALL

SPECIAL THANKS
ULA MOS, COREY KNAEBEL
NEI RUFFINO, KATE FINNEGAN

COVER CREDITS
FICO OSSIO, ERIC BASALDUA,
JEN BROOMALL, MIKE DEBALFO,
JEFF PINA, RENATO REI,
COREY KNAEBEL

CHARACTER DESIGNS

TOM HUTCHISON - ADAM WITHERS - FICO OSSIO

JEN BROOMALL

CRITTER VOL 3, October 2013. Published by Big Dog Ink. Office of publication: 2301 Wing St, Rolling Meadows IL 60008. Copyright © 2013 Tom Hutchison. All rights reserved. CRITTER (including all prominent characters featured herin), it's logo and all character likenesses are trademarks of Tom Hutchison unless otherwise noted. No part of this publication may be reproduced or transmitted, in any form or by any means (except for short exerpts for review purposes) without the express written permission of Tom Hutchison. All names, characters, events and locales in this publication are entirely fictional. Any resemblence to actual persons (living or dead), events or places, without satiric intent, is coincidental.

Interesting Fact: Penny for Your Soul, which was the first book I ever published, was originally planned to spin off from Critter. The Las Vegas crossover you see in this book was going to be my way of introducing the demons and angels and situations of what was to be my second book to my current fans. But things do not always go exactly as planned and Penny for Your Soul was released

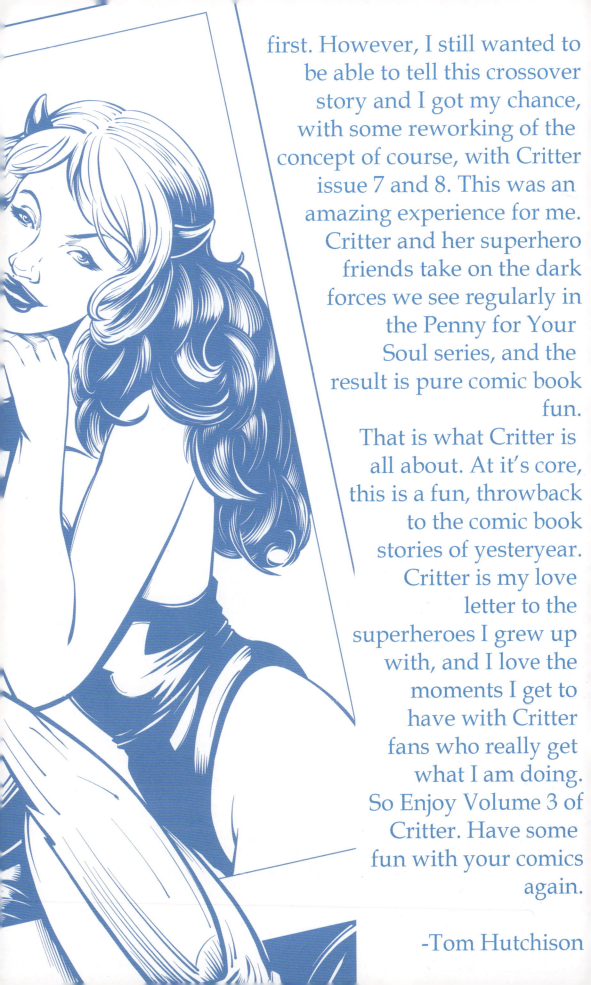

first. However, I still wanted to be able to tell this crossover story and I got my chance, with some reworking of the concept of course, with Critter issue 7 and 8. This was an amazing experience for me. Critter and her superhero friends take on the dark forces we see regularly in the Penny for Your Soul series, and the result is pure comic book fun.

That is what Critter is all about. At it's core, this is a fun, throwback to the comic book stories of yesteryear. Critter is my love letter to the superheroes I grew up with, and I love the moments I get to have with Critter fans who really get what I am doing. So Enjoy Volume 3 of Critter. Have some fun with your comics again.

-Tom Hutchison

PLEASE SIGN HERE, AND WE'LL TAKE CARE OF HIM.

SO LISTEN, WE APPRECIATE THE ASSISTANCE THE SUPER HERO COMMUNITY PROVIDES US, BUT *THIS* GUY IS A BIT ON THE SMALL POTATOES SIDE. MAYBE YOU SHOULD CONCENTRATE ON SOME OF THE MORE *DIFFICULT* BAD GUYS.

YOU'RE KIDDING, RIGHT?

WADDAYA THINK I'VE BEEN DOING?

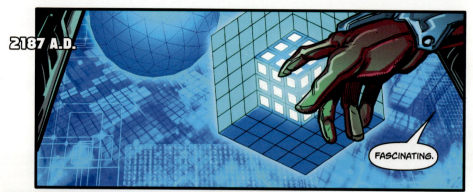

Who's Who
In the Critter Universe

Muskrat
n environmentalist do-gooder who auses more harm than good.

Flamingo
A classically trained dancer who puts her skills to work in the criminal underworld.

Iron Butterfly
A young girl in a pink and purple suit of armor, with a set of real butterfly wings.

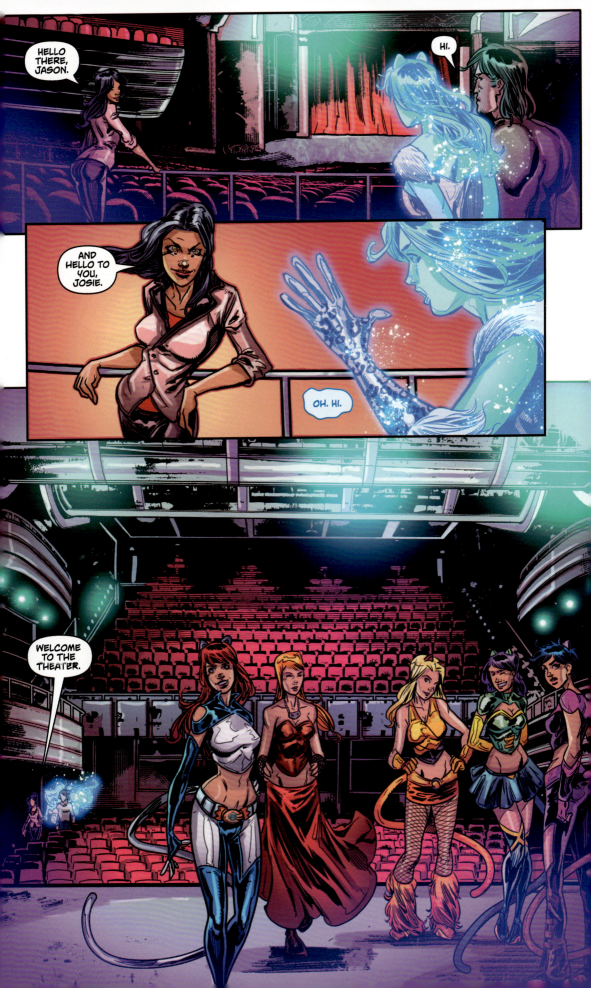

Who's Who
In the Critter Universe

The Apprentice

An illusionist who uses pages of the Necronomicon to conjur spirits.

Black Collars

Mystic cult who's sole purpose is enslave the world using the pages of the Necronomicon.

Jezebel

One of history's most notorious women and the current Babylon Hotel manager.

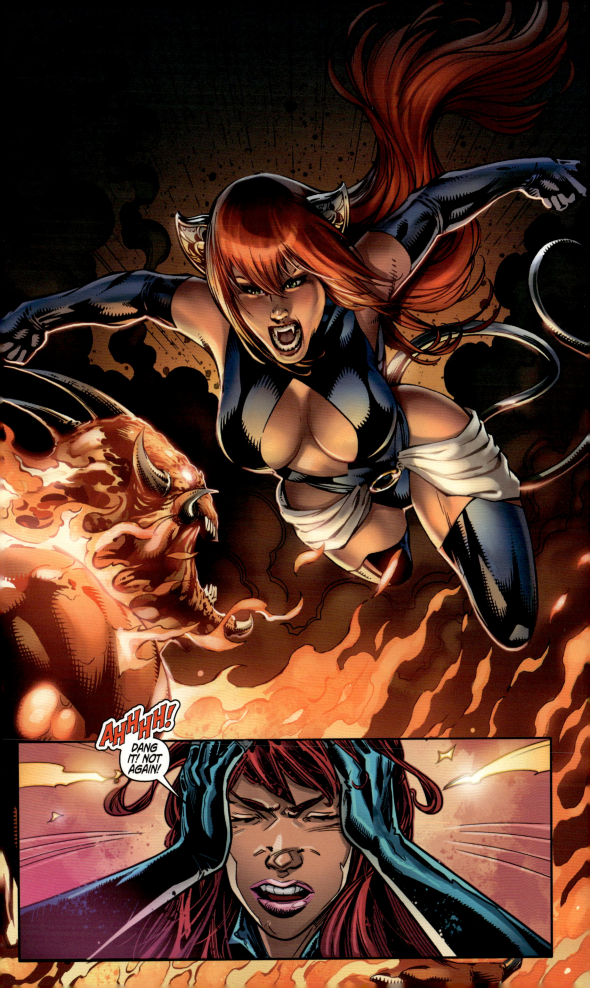

Who's Who
In the Critter Universe

Danica
The owner of the Babylon Hotel in Las Vegas also happens to be the granddaughter of the Devil, Lucifer himself. She buys the souls of her unsuspecting patrons for $10,000!

Ronnie
Manager of the Superpawn pawn shop for heroes and villains. Loves his job...mostly.

Who's Who
In the Critter Universe

Brawn

heroic powerhouse. rawn looks for the ations many other roes can't handle

School Girl I

Former Purrrfection member, Kitten, has decided to become the world's smartest hero.

Mrs. Glenridge

Mother of the deceased super hero, Josie, who has a few secrets of her own to keep quiet.

SCHOOL GIRL

SCHOOL GIRL HAS QUICKLY BECOME A FAN FAVORITE CHARACTER, AND WHY NOT?

CUTE, SPUNKY AND WITH TAG LINES THAT SOME SUPER HEROES CAN ONLY DREAM OF.

WHEN IT CAME TIME TO DESIGN HER LOOK, WE DIDN'T WANT TO FALL INTO THE TRAP OF HAVING HER LOOK LIKE THE STEREOTYPICAL SCHOOL GIRL WE ALL KNOW. SO JEN BROOMALL WAS GIVEN THE CHALLENGE OF CREATING A YOUTHFUL COSTUME WITH FUN DETAILS, BUT WITHOUT THE OVER SEXUALIZED STANDARD THAT THE OUTFIT GENERALLY RECEIVES.

MISSION ACCOMPLISHED.

SKETCH GALLERY & CONCEPT DESIGNS

APPRENTICE

THE APPRENTICE IS ALL ABOUT THE LAS VEGAS SHOW GIRL WORLD, AND SHE PULLS IT OFF PERFECTLY.

SHE WAS ORIGINALLY DESIGNED TO BE A STAPLE CHARACTER FOR THE CRITTER UNIVERSE, BUT HER ORIGIN STORY CLEARLY WAS A BETTER FIT FOR THE PENNY FOR YOUR SOUL WORLD.

THOSE WORLDS COLLIDED IN A TWO PART CROSSOVER STORY, OF COURSE, AND SO OUR LAS VEGAS MAGICIAN GOT HER CHANCE TO BE THE CONNECTING PIECE OF THE BDI UNIVERSE.

SKETCH GALLERY & CONCEPT DESIGNS

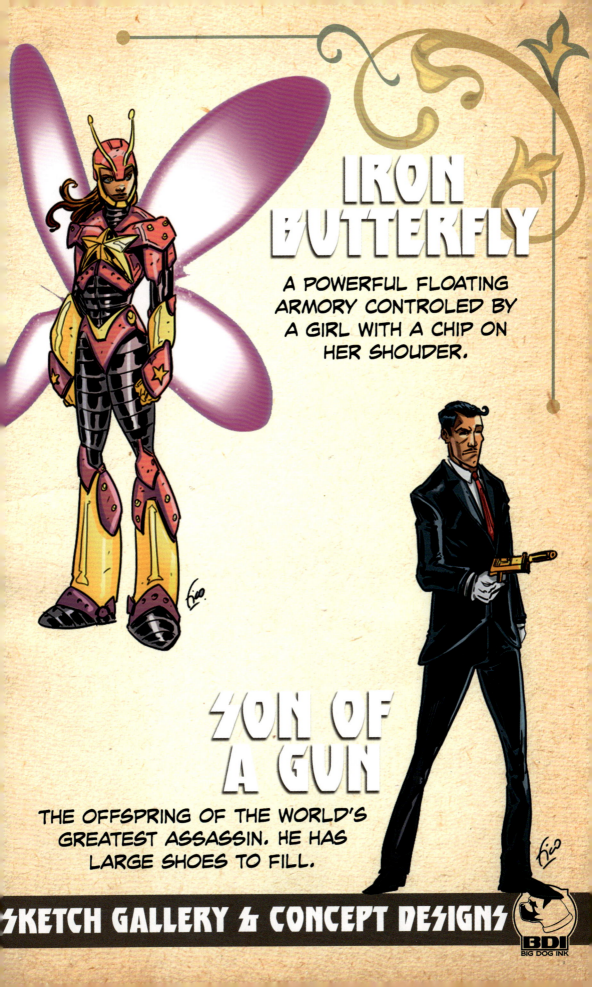